HE IS STILL MINE

TANYA VATSA

ISBN 979-888606596-1

To my parents,

who believed in me and gave me the strength to choose my own dreams.

Contents

Foreword

The only reason for being in pain, feeling broken and not letting myself heal is the fear of losing every part of you in seconds, the part of you which still resides in me,

Preface

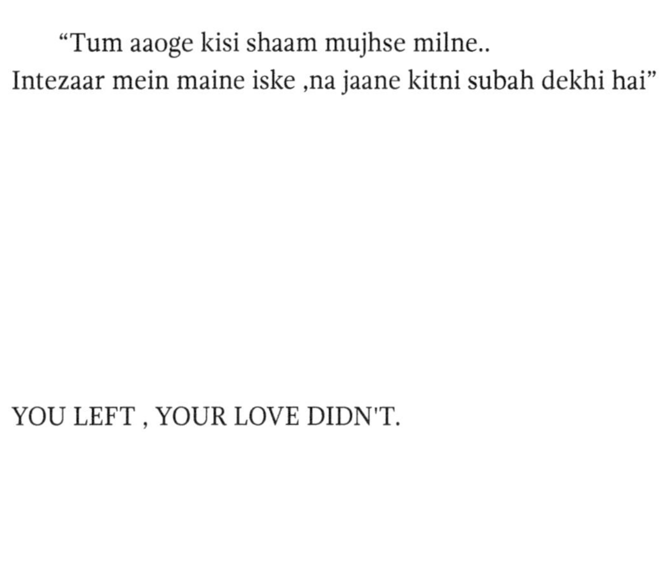

"Tum aaoge kisi shaam mujhse milne..
Intezaar mein maine iske ,na jaane kitni subah dekhi hai"

YOU LEFT , YOUR LOVE DIDN'T.

A fictional tale.. but some of it actually happened.

Acknowledgements

Before I continue..

It was never easy to write this book. The journey was never easy. When I decided to republish this book, I was scared. I never thought I would be able to do this without you all.

To all my people, who stood beside me in my worst phases and celebrated all my victories together.

To the one who discovered a writer within me. I won't have written this without you. Thankyou for believing in my passion and being my best cheerleader always.

To my parents , my mom and dad Dr. Rekha Kumari and Dr. Rajeev Kumar who made me strong enough to choose my career. Thanks for believing in me.

To my brother Hemant Jha for being there for me always.

To, Pranavi Mishra for being my home and setting up the fire in my soul. I won't have ever thought of doing this.

Ananya for loving me unconditionally.

Shreya and Prishiyas for being the first editors of the book.

Samyak for re- designing the beautiful cover.

Last but not the least to all my cousins, my friends, my family members. It's not easy for me to mention all of you here, but thanks to you for bearing with my impatience.

Without you all this book won't come up.

Prologue

Distance is always shown as a symbol, which brings two lovers closer, but is it really so?My love for him can never be portrayed with the metaphors I write in my poems.

What's love? My heart questioned? Was it when my heart skipped a beat? Was it when I looked with the same emotions even when he left?

This story is about Ruhan and Anika.

Ruhan, a young boy who was full of life. The one person anyone could fall in love with.

Anika, a girl with dreams in her eyes and passion in her heart.

Everyone does have a story. I am sure you will find one story once you start reading it.Will they meet again? The story of memories, confession, nostalgia and heartbreak.

With the fragrance of the last letter I wrote for my lover....

CHAPTER ONE

A NEW BEGINING

It was Tuesday, 12th April.
I still remember the date very well. Summer was on its peak. I was getting ready, busy arranging my books, searching for my pen and HC VERMA together. I don't know why but this always happens to me, I never find my things one at a time.

Mom was already shouting. I still had to get ready.
You know, sometimes it's the universe who even gives you a sign but we humans are so busy, we fail to notice it.

I too failed to notice it. You might be thinking what was it. You definitely will find everything inside.

Searching for my beige-coloured ripped jeans and t-shirt, made me already late for my class. Finally a new chapter was about to begin. I don't know why but I could feel both, serotonin and adrenaline rush in my body.

First day of my coaching. I was excited to start a new journey of my life.
I had decided to pursuc biology (PCB), and was aiming to get admission in a medical college.

I still don't understand why people give extra emphasis on asking their children to pursue science. I was always into arts, but being an intelligent student my society did not let me pursue it. So, I chose to opt for biology. I am glad now people are much more understanding, and yes they have stopped discriminating subjects .

Also now my parents are happy with the things I do in my life.

You know you never value anything until it brings a drastic change in your life. Alone in my room while I regretted for years for not choosing ARTS, now I feel satisfied. They say, everyone loves the spring until you fall in love in autumn.

Had I not opted for the subject, I would have not met him. Life is unpredictable. You never know what's coming your way. Life makes you experience all the crazy things you decide not to be a part of.

Coming back to the year 2015, I had just finished my board exams. Results were yet to come. It's always a smart decision to start early. So instead of exploring more and taking a break for a few months. I decided to live at home and prepare from here itself, closing all the family discussion over going to Kota.

That day, late in afternoon , the sun was really blazing up , and it was intolerable. I was already late. Suddenly , the weather changed , the sun started to play hide and seek and clouds covered up all the sky into its arms. I think nature was giving me a sign writing up a start of a beautiful journey.

I had never written a poem before , I have always loved reading since I was a child. Reading stories always delighted me. I tried to write several stories before but could not succeed.

That day was different. I could feel a vibe, something was about to happen.

As I walked down the streets, My mind started to hymn poetry.

The language of my love,
Was portrayed as one
We learnt in literature in school days,
back when Romeo Juliet flattered around my heart.

I don't know why I sang a love poem. Writing poetries on love was never my genre. Love to me was an illusion. It's like waiting for water near the oasis. I never hated the idea of falling in love but I was scared to fall in love.

Do you even remember,
The game of F-L-A-M-E-S?
Where the last pages has holds, scratches,
Oh yes smiles too for you to be my love.
My cheeks blushing around, turning red
Drenching me in a delusion,
Blurring the scenes, traffic sounds, all what is there making me learn the 5 signs of Rafaqat / Companionship

I have always tried to believe in adrenaline and dopamine but that day before I reached my coaching, I finished writing a poem, that too a loved one, tuning the rhythms perfectly in my mind.

I hold to love you , for as life still beautiful
With the aroma all around, waiting again to see you,
With my fingers crossed, when it's dark all around,
Listening to Lag Jaa Gale, of love and separation,
Asking for a star to fall from universe,
Stopping just to make a wish.
I never told you, but I want you to stay.

With ending my poetry, oh yes a loved one,
had reached my destination, from where it all began, the journey of finding a friend, a lover and a companion.

Love is an unparalleled feeling in the world. Suddenly the words and phrases aren't enough to describe the beauty of your lover. It's undeniable that love changes you as a person, it certainly does. On lonely nights, you befriend metaphors and everything starts to make sense. Their face is like the moon, stealing the darkness from the night and filling up your life with hope and light. Their eyes are like the deep blue ocean you love yourself to drown in and reach to the bottom to unravel the mysteries, one after another. Their lips are like the petals of roses, every time you kiss you plant a piece of yours in them. Love grows eventually, sometimes it takes days, months, or even years to fathom its extremity.

I was already 20 minutes late and was already struggling to find a seat. My physics teacher saw my struggle to search for a seat and asked the boy in the pink shirt to shift a little more. so that I could make my place.

I was relieved to find a seat on the first bench. We as students always become more responsible when it comes to the competitive exams. It gets quite tough. Life is never just a struggle to find a solution between two linear particles, but it does bring you happiness if everytime you get a correct solution. (The idea of finding solutions always excites me a bit)

He started to teach us unit and dimension , (the real struggle every science student faces) . I was very happy because I had already revised it and could easily answer. (now, don't think I was a teacher's pet)

My classes got over and I followed the steps back to my home. I didn't think much of the boy who sat next to me.

We were on the same bench for 3 hours, and on my way I barely thought about him. On my way back home, I was just struggling to remember the piece of poetry I wrote. I wanted to pen it down in my diary.

I used to write everything in my diary. My poems were not mere words, or prose, it always had been an escape to write down my secrets easily through words on a piece of paper.

CHAPTER TWO

THE LITTLE CONVERSATION

Have you ever felt the soft kiss on your forehead, or someone sliding their fingers to fix the gap your hand holds? Have you ever felt someone's touch being so vibrant that it nestles away the pain your lonely soul is going through. It's said one gets crazy when they fall in love but the only thing I wish to confess to my lover is about how I have grown up in love, and how beautifully my pain swamped away wrapping me up in lillies around.

Love is like magic. It not only tempts your heart, but bewitches your soul too. With each passing day, you are carried slowly, and you tread reveries to keep afloat.

2 weeks passed by. I used to notice him. I knew he noticed me too sometimes. We never tried to have a conversation. I still don't know why it takes us so long to begin a conversation. Maybe, because we knew someday or another this would begin.

AFTER 2 WEEKS, he finally decided to start a conversation

April, 26 2015. 18.54. (I still remember the date and time)

"Hii..
I am Ruhan.."

"Heyy

Anika here...."

So our first conversation began. Though it began formally, we vibed up with each other quite well and in no time. We started our discussion over theories, taught in our physics class, mole concept, which screwed both of our minds very quickly.

There was something in his voice which was quite soothing. It gave butterflies in my stomach. It was different. Butterflies in my stomach and fireflies in my soul.

The feeling was different. It was like a love poem weaving around and I was ready to listen to it for my complete life even if it would destroy me and my existence completely.

His eyes were just like a puzzle, making me confused and amazed both at the same time. I knew, I always knew he and I were different. This was never meant to be, but sometimes you even desire to kill yourself, leaving yourself on the verge of self destruction.

There was something in his eyes. A void, and I had decided to solve it. It was for the first time, my priorities changed.

You sometimes try to condemn your feelings of possessiveness, suppressing the emotions, the emotions symphonically naming it as mere hormonal balance. But when your heart skips a beat every time you hear their voice, the adrenaline rush never lets you blame it all on hormones. There's a galaxy in your soul craving to find your only moon, for they shine a little brighter making you feel completely the same as it feels when you see a constellation.

"Where do you see yourself in next three years", he asked
"I probably see myself in a medical college pursuing M.B.B.S in next three years if everything goes according to the plan.

(But when has everything gone according to the plan in anybody's life?)

I asked the same question and a never ending conversation began between us.

The three hours became the best part of my complete day. With him, I didn't have to fake this. It was easy to be the real Anika.

Love tips toes when you expect the least in your life. With him I started to overcome my weakness. My heart was radiant, ready to beat a little faster as soon as someone would call his name.

It was drenching and even when I knew the pain of heartbreak wouldn't be an easy journey, I decided to set it free, in the name of love, trust and an eternal faith.

2nd May, 2015

"Have you revised 'Chemical Bonding'?"

"Aaj test hai yaar , aur maine kuch nahi padha hai", he said.

"Don't worry , I am done with the chapter and will help you", I said.

"Yaar tum bolti bhi ho"?, he asked

"Haan"

"Yes"

"I speak and speak a lot to people who are my friends and so, you might have not seen me talking more often.", I said

The test was moderate, helped him to solve the questions, which he doubtedly believed, hoping I am giving him the right answers, cross checking it with other students.

I don't know why he had such trust issues, with the answers, it was just a weekly test.

"You know we are really a good match – you are a very good listener, and I speak a lot", he winked.

When the contracting valves try to summon up the feelings, the one which brought fireflies all around, making you realise about the rusted emotions bragging along like a heavy bag, they bring calmness to your chaos.

Love demands courage and when you know the person may never love you back it takes ounce of strength to kneel down on your knees praying for their happiness.
I was never into these cheesy lines but with him everything was different. I never had such a friend. He used to understand me the way no one could . (My best friend is going to disown me after reading this).

In all our spare time, we were always together. I didn't use any social media nor did I have a personal mobile, still the three hours were enough to know amusing things about each other

CHAPTER THREE

FOUR LETTER WORD: LOVE

It was three weeks since I and Ruhan started talking.There was something even Ruhan didn't know about his ownself.He used to be lost in the haze of silence.

Have you ever seen the moon kissing the waves of the ocean, lighting the water giving it glitters to shine in the perfect starry night? Love gives you the same feeling that it's true. Each night when you relax yourself on the corner of shore, enjoying the sound of waves kissing your feelings, muting the noise, the one person you think about is them.

Though, I never thought it's a strong feeling and I could never think of giving this feeling a name. I have always loved reading those 26 alphabet , still calling this with the four letter word, LOVE was never easy. Me

It was three weeks later, we were now good friends.Our friendship and syllabus both were going hand in hand.Our Studies caught up a speed. Daily practice papers, weekly tests made their place in our daily life.

It was monday,still we had a holiday.Getting a holiday in a week day was always a relief.

I thought about revising numericals.(Biology walon ka real struggle yahan se shuru hota hai).

While checking my notes out, I found his copy in my bag. At first I thought to just keep it safely with me but then I don't know why I thought to turn the pages of his copy.

I know this is wrong but I have a habit, I get curious to see what's scribbled on their last pages.

I started turning the last pages of his notebook and while turning the pages, I found all the rough works which was very expected, but what I did not expect were those short
4- liners, some which held unheard stories, those lines which were complete, still incomplete.

This was my first ever uneconomic friendship with a boy, I do not know much about him yet, still I knew a lot about him. Our bond touched bases on various things, our hobbies ,our dreams, those passions, the movies I loved watching, things that excited him and many more.

I really liked talking to him, with him time used to pass in seconds, and without him even seconds used to pass like days.

His sense of humour would make my jaw ache. I used to laugh all the time I used to be with him and these four- liners were too sad for his personality and I really wanted to know why it holds the sadness,which I could sense.

In these few months, I did all the things which I never expected from me.

I wrote a love poem for the first time in my whole lifetime, I talked to a boy forgetting my ego, those and now I wanted to complete that four liner and wanted to know the story behind it.

I still remember the four liner he wrote.

"I am not all here today,
Drowning in my past,
Drenched with thoughts,
Sorrows that forever last."

And thought to complete it.

"There are questions
Floating in my head,
Breathing but not alive,
Lifeless yet not dead.

.

Desolate and broken,
Missing out the zeal.
Desires and passion,
Hard to conceal."

I couldn't sleep that very whole night. The next day I waited for him to come to class. It was for the first time, I regretted not having my personal mobile. If that day I would have my phone, I would have called him up and asked the question, "what is the thing you are going through"?

"What is worrying you"?

I was just wondering why I was so tense but probably found no answers to it and I did not need any answers.

I was worried and that's okay.

It was 4.00 AM in the morning and sleep was nowhere in my eyes. I just kept looking at the ceiling fan, thinking about rotational motion but could not focus on it, getting my thoughts converging again being converged about Ruhan. That night I couldn't even blink my eyes,waiting only for time to run faster.

The struggle was real. I was tensed for someone I just met a month ago. He was my good friend but was he just a good friend?

Finally controlling my mind I made myself calm, and waited for the night to end.

I never skipped my food before , that too for someone else, No, never.

I didn't know what was happening with me. My brain was trying to make out peace but my heart wanted to see him, hear his voice.

"What happened to you"? Are you okay? Say whatever you want to ".?

These questions were running all in my mind.

I couldn't see him slipping out in depression, even though I wasn't sure that he was really depressed for real?

Or maybe not? But I just wanted to talk to him. My gut feeling said he wasn't okay.

He came to the coaching and I just bursted out myself, giving my desperacy a silent slap.

"Are you okay? Is anything bothering you? Is something depressing you? Or Is it just a four liner"?, I asked

It took him some minutes to realise what is happening

I recited the 4 liner he wrote and then he said, laughingly, "Were you really worried? About me.?"

“Leave the jokes aside and tell me the real thing.You know what I couldn't sleep the whole night, thinking about it, and here again," I became impatient.

He again used it as his weapon making me clean bold, asking me just one single question,

" What made you sleepless, why were you so worried, is it just a four liner "?, and it made me speechless.

"Listen, you are really my good friend. I don't want to lose you. You look cute when you smile."

"And when I don't,? ", he asked jokingly

"Yaar mai sach me pareshan hu"? Tu samaj nahi raha? "

" Ani, I am okay, there are some issues going on in my life and I was really worried about the same. I don't like writing poems, but poems heals me. ", he said with a soft heart.

" yaar , I love reading poems, stories, and you know what you write really well. I tried to complete the poem you wrote.", I continued reciting the poem.

" You are such a sweetheart, " he held my hand. Don't leave me ever. You are a friend I can't ever lose", and he just got numbed.

CHAPTER FOUR

FOOTPRINTS OF LOVE

You know it's never easy to talk about your trauma. There are things which trigger you but you need to be silent. Why? Why can't we scream?

We humans always find reasons. Ruhan was also looking for one . An escape or a home. He thought he could handle it but even running away from those memories never worked well either

"Ani"

"Sometimes I really wish to scream, but cannot.."

" Every person has some likes and dislikes. But when it comes to depression, sadness, people think it's a thing to gain attention. I am not depressed but yes, I needed someone to share my things."

"I have lots of friends, I study, I talk, and even flirt with girls, like you have always seen me smiling, they have the same image of me, but it was just you who could see the pain."

"My parents don't live here, I live here all alone. There are times when I need people, but I understand dad has his office and my boards hold me back here. Banaras is a beautiful city and I love this city."

"You know what I like about it most?..

He was telling me about his story and I was lost listening to him.

“I like these streets, it tells about the love, the solitude is peace. These ghats, I love sitting here for hours there. Banaras gives me peace and I even found a best girl-friend here".

"Girlfriend? ", I asked

"Haan you?"

"Me? "

"Yes.? You are a girl. And you are my friend. So you are my girlfriend”.

“Hai na? ", he asked smilingly.

"You and your lines"

“Uff” .I smiled back

“And I mean it. I promise I won’t ever leave you alone.You aren’t alone.", I promised.

"And promises are meant to be kept".. I retaliated, and he smiled back.

"Absolutely!”, “I know you won’t break your promise.”, he said smilingly.

This was another landmark in our friendship, and henceforth it made our bond strong.

And I felt good, because he was okay. He was smiling.
And finally the reason was me. I was feeling so good. I was happy. And just his smile made me feel so good as if I have achieved everything. But something within me wanted this to last for a long time.. Forever.

We became friends. Then best friends. It was never love at the first sight. But there were feelings which were building up. Were we getting close? Sounds crazy? Right!

There are times when your heart becomes vulnerable to love someone without any expectations, any hopes deep inside it wants that love back, making all those wrong deeds right, embracing and cherishing the memories, giving you an ecstasy of dreams. There are times when you want to focus on other things, but all your heart needs is their presence, right beside you. Being with them just makes everything perfect.

Getting back to my own story. I still didn't have a mobile or a social media but we used to spend time in class, after class, solving questions together, fighting for pen, teasing each other, or sometimes I just used to stare at him.

I didn't know what love is. This was a new feeling for me and it felt good. He made me discover the version of myself, which I never thought to know of.

Sitting in the class alone, I used to smile.

Everyone in the class could sense it, but we could not. I was getting a different feeling but wasn't easily ready to accept that it's love. (I think most of you can relate to it).

He never wished to confess. I never wished to accept. We both knew it, but denial was on its peak.

Love was in the air.
Our story was a different one.
It had turns, it had twists. We used to fight but still I couldn't live without listening to his voice.

To fall in love is easy, but when you fall in love, commitment and promises come with it parallely. And relationships always fades from love.

To fall in love is easy,and I fell in love, in love with my best friend, but I wasn't ready to accept it.

I used to tell his stories to all my friends. Everyone who knew me, now knew him, who he was and what he meant to me, except the person who actually should know about it.

(Trust me, pyaar karna aasan hota hai ,izhaar karna nahi)

I was commitment phobic, what if he breaks friendship, what if he doesn't reciprocate the same feelings, whenever I decide to confess everything to him, these questions won't allow me to confess it.

It wasn't easy. But thanks to my 11th result, I scored third rank and was given a mobile, Samsung J1 Ace.

You know why I believe in destiny, we both didn't had smartphone and we both got it at the same time.

We had lots of similarities, which indicated that we have a story to live. A story till eternity. It's like destiny already wrote a story, deciding the characters.

I got my mobile, but you know what's worse? Before I could connect with him anywhere, take his number, confess my love, our batches got reshuffled.

I had no contact to get in touch with him but without him even studies seemed boring.

(don't forget I was a NEET aspirant).

I literally had just one friend in my class and, yes okay now I loved him but without him everything seemed empty.

I was thinking too much. Much more than my heart could handle. With each day passing by I was really missing him badly.

I was slowly falling in love with him everyday, a battle was going between my heart and my mind. I wished him back, just in the moment.

In his absence I realised he now holded much of me. He resided in me more than I lived in myself.

I was still waiting. But love is not easy, it comes with hurdles, battles, barriers and you need to fight. Thankfully I wasn't alone, My best friend was all the way here with me.

(Remember , I mentioned her right in the beginning of my story).

Ruhani, my childhood friend, we have been friends for more than 17 years and believe me we have not just spent years we have lived each other's life together.

I don't tell this usually but she means a lot to me. She has been with me on days when no one else was. She knew my condition. She was the one who went to the coaching authority pleading to shuffle us too, in the reshuffled batch, giving excuse of time.

Our coaching was strict and it wasn't easy, as easy as we felt it would be. But after an hour of requesting them, we were finally shifted into the batch, the batch where my heart resided

(The shifting was not easy.There's a long story behind it. It's for me to know and you to guess).

I was so happy that if it would not be my educational institution I would have danced without music for hours. I could sing loudly or even do something more crazy, I could scream out his name loudly.

I was waiting for Tuesday to come. Meanwhile I realised its been one year of journey, but it wasn't still easy to confess my love.

"See I have done lots of struggle to get you into this batch. You will now have to confess it to him. Or else I will say out all your feelings".. Ruhani blackmailed me.

"Hey hey.. Miss Radio, stop stop", I calmed her out and promised to confess my feelings.

You know I have always mentioned destiny because it's really important in my life. I wanted Ruhan's number and saw I got the same batch, a seat again next to him.

When I entered the coaching, I could literally see his face, he was shocked to see me, and I was just awestruck at that moment, all things around me got blurred, I was just staring at him and I couldn't keep my eyes away. I was draining in the moment, my heart beats were so high that if he would be near me he could have felt it. I just wanted to hold him tightly and say all what I was waiting to spill out things and speak my heart out.

(Normally heart beats sound like lub-dub, lub -dub my was screaming Ruhan, Ruhan).

(It's normal right ? Aap sabke saath bhi hua hoga)

I kept staring at him, it was embarrassing. I know, still, this was my moment. I have waited for it for such a long time.

I got a seat next to him, after all it was my place and even my person. Okay not still? But still he was mine.. Only mine.

CHAPTER FIVE

NEW LOVE STORY IN THE CITY

"Ani ,see I got a new phone", he jumped

"Arreyy I got a new phone too" , I now played my inning.

“Hey would you mind sharing me your number?”, he asked

Thing I wanted him to ask for and my answer came very quick ,

“No no, not at all”

I dialed up my number in his phone and got his number in my phone.

Love has struggles, and my struggle began from here.

I got a phone, playing the password game was tough.

I could not save his number by the name of a boy. It wasn’t easy those days.

And there again my girl came to my rescue, she suggested me the name of a girl and then Ruhan became (whatever let’s ignore), what’s important is I finally got his number.

He was never my crush. I wasn’t ever attracted to him. I was always attached, an attachment that holded my heart in such a way, like some barren lands are poured up with drops of rain.

Once in a lifetime, you meet someone, someone more than friend, more than a lover, someone who is mate to your soul, someone with whom life seems to be full of colours and rainbow, and I found that someone in him.

We got connected on WhatsApp with a condition, he won't ever keep his picture as his display picture, although I Just made Facebook to stalk his Facebook pictures.

It was 8.00 PM. I remember when he texted me a first hii and I was unable to wait even for a while I replied back.
(Aur yahan mein pighal gayi)

The second text he sent me was I missed you so much , thank god you came, what would have I done without you.

I promised you that I won't leave you alone ever, so how could I.

Don't you trust me.

Ani.. Let's promise each other whatever be the situation we won't leave each other alone. We will be best friends for life long.

Yes, best friends.

That was all , I was with him .
I Never knew this best friend word would hurt this much.

But he wasn't my friend. I was sure of it. As sure as I am of the fact that the sun rises in the east.

But now I was more scared to confess. I couldn't lose him. And what if my confession ruins it all.

It was the beginning of August. Almost a year and half had passed since we first met, but still now my heart wasn't able to resist my love for him.

I couldn't handle friendship when I was so in love with him. His every word touched my heart.

I decided to write something and send it. And just started to type,

Love holds emotions.
It's not just about feelings.
It's about the emotions of both partners, care they show ,the fights, the arguments, loyalty,insecurities, jealousy, but above all holding each other's hand till eternity.
It's about making a journey from one's heart to other's soul.

Love changes people . Even when you know the person you love is never going to come to you , the person will never love you back but still the heart wants to give it a try.

The heart still tries to do everything just to make that person smile.

It's their smile which makes you drive more crazy .

You start feeling all sorts of sensations and the smile makes your heart rain and their smiles are the perfect rainbow in front of your eyes.

If the person cherishes your soul, If you feel that these are the hands you search for when your fingers are cold , if you search for them when you are sad , if you find yourself onto him/her

Believe me you have found the love of your life.

Believe me if you have found the love of your life it's the best blessing you have found.

I wrote the text and thought of backspace and mistakenly clicked on the send button.

If it would be 2019, I would have deleted the text, but it was 2016 and WhatsApp does not have any such options there.

"So who stole your heart Miss Ani"..? He asked

Probably no one, it's just a scribbling, I texted back

So from when you started scribbling all these?, he texted again.

"Actually."

I wrote and left

"Oh C'mon na.. Tell na who's the one.," he asked

"Why can't you tell me? I am your best friend."

I wanted to share but how could I.

I still kept numb.

And thought to write something hinting him out he is the one.

The rainy days,
The thundering lights,
The tulips, the daisies,
The tempting vibes.

Tired soul,
Messy life,
As if you, me and it were just a lie.

Broken enough into pieces,
Shattered as the glass jar,
Holding all in my hand,
Kissing all my scars.
Scared enough to love again,
Scared to hold onto you
Still in love,
Ain't not able to forget you.
All strings detached,
Still attached on your things,
Yet in love with you,
A boy who never noticed me.
The girl who is hurt,
The girl who is bold,
The girl who is vibrant,
Will all her heart be cold.
The girl who you never noticed,
The girl you never loved,
The girl who walked away,
The girl who silently cried,
The girl who loved you,
The girl who slowly died.

I sent

And he read it.

Typing.. It showed

(Have you ever waited for your boards result?You know how nervous it makes you ,I was nervous as same)

"See Ani.. I am feeling there's something in your heart. Tell na. We have promised each other that we won't hide anything", he typed

"Yes, exactly we are best friends. Right?", I sent

(Sarcasm.. ;))

Yes, we are...but are we just friends Ani?, he asked

Probably no, but you won't understand, so leave it. I typed and backspaced.

"Yes., We are best friends," I typed.

I wanted to confess, but every time I thought of saying these things, I remembered his words and my heart would get fragile.

"Ani, you are my friend. You are a girl I have noticed and thought of as ``friendship" .I received the text and thought not to hide my feelings this time.

"Listen Ruhan", I sent

I started typing..

"You are my best friend. You have been the best thing that has ever happened to me. You have made me believe what love really is. I have feelings for you and I feel it's better to say it , so yes for me it's more than friendship.

I love you so much Ruhan.

It's okay if you don't and it's okay if you don't want to keep the friendship.

But I couldn't hide my feelings now."

I typed and decided to be offline.

CHAPTER SIX

THE UNEXPECTED PROPOSAL

Love never searches out for a tag. It's never about relationships, rather it's about acceptance. To love is easy but to accept someone with all the flaws, that's what it demands for. It's eternal. It's about being happy even if you are going through the worst phase of your life. In those days when you don't even want to talk, their voice makes you feel like home. It resonates with your soul, finding their essence of fragrance in your life.

I received a call. A call from him.

" Hello" , I said with a trembling voice.

"Are you crying?
Anii yaar, why do you think I don't feel the same" .

"I don't know," I said cryingly, trying to control the tears.

"But I love you and it's love. I just love you, and this can't be changed."

"Neither I nor you nor someone else."

"Arey.. Baba", he tried to console.

"Can I get a minute"?, he asked

And continued

"In the name of God, my family and you ,Anika, I Ruhan confesses I love you, just you with all the core of my heart", and will keep loving you forever."

I felt I was dreaming, my dreams were coming true. If 11.11 wishes are ever listened to then I will say, he was my 11.11 wish, unexpected yet beautiful, the one who brought all the smile, fragrance and light in my life.

Earlier I used to breathe, his entry in my life, made me live my life to the fullest.

Time changes people but we started to grow in love. We needed no one. We were enough for each other. We used to sing together, study together, eat together all over a phone call.

We used to discuss our dreams, our passion, our marriage, our life, earlier we used to share our own dreams but now there was no I, no you ,we were we.

We used to make promises, we used to share smiles, the cries, we used to fight but at last we were always together.

We used to discuss everything, those romantic chats, those stupid things we did, everything.

Many nights we just used to sing his favourite song together and sleep over a call.

"Mai tenu samjhawan ki..
Na tere bina lagda jee.."

"Anni, keep your hair open when you come to class, you look beautiful" , he used to demand silly cute things from me.

October that year..

"Hiii Babu," I called him, with a pinch of passion that night.

"Heya mera bacha", he used to say.

Mera baccha would melt my heart and I wished to go to him and hold him all in my arms, so tight that I can hear his breath.

"Do you know what's tomorrow"? I asked

"Haan.. It's my shona's birthday" and I want you to spend all your time with yours.

"Me, my time, all is yours", I blushingly replied.

"I have a surprise for you. After the class ends, come to the terrace, alone" , he said laughingly.

I want you to spend all your time with me, just me and you.

It was my birthday. But he was more excited than I was.

He was waiting for me on the terrace.

I and Ruhan got lots of time to spend together. But this day was different. It was our first date.

I was very excited for the moment. I wore his favourite red top, with crimson cream ankle length jeans. opened up my hair, because he loved me with open hairs.

I wore small studs in my ear.I I don't know why I was so conscious of my look all of a sudden. It was never about looks. We were in love, in love with each other's soul, but when you are in love, you start caring for yourself a little more.

I went directly to the terrace after the classes got over. He was waiting for me. As I came in front of him, he touched my face, that adrenaline rush was so real. The fingers on my face made me blush a little more. I was just getting hypnotised into the moment. His beautiful eyes, how cannot someone get lost into them. Those fingers made me look more beautiful just by touching my face. I just closed my eyes and was living the moment. It was beautiful. I wanted to freeze it. Just hold onto it.

I was all lost in him. Still I couldn't believe it.

"Happy birthday my love".., he came closer to me and whispered it slowly in my ears.

It was a wonderful moment. We were with each other holding each other's hand. He decorated a corner of the terrace, with some of those white fairy lights. The moon was shining brightly and when the moonlight kissed his face, he would look more adorable, someone I could stare at the whole night.

But time, it never stops. When you want to hold, it passes more fastly.

"You know I love you so much", he said holding my hand tightly. We sat in the corner playing with the fingers, and then lost the fingers entangled in each other's hand. I wished to hold his hand forever. I rested my chin on his shoulder.

He tucked my hair behind my ears.

"This is beautiful", I said.

Sometimes I lose my own emotions. I just couldn't believe he was mine, just mine.

I grabbed his arm and held him all, I was close to him, close enough to hear those warm breaths and I realised I was in love with his every flaw, his soul, his smile, everything.

He brought me up a pastry, my favourite flavour, butterscotch. I blew up the candle and he kept singing for me, the happy birthday song.

I felt blessed to have him in my life.

"Okay bye, for now. It's 8, I need to go. Mom would get worried about where I am", I said

I got up to leave and he hold my wrist from behind. I wish I could stop, but the moment couldn't be freezed.

"Wait, just for a minute", he said

"Where are you going,?", he asked

bachha I need to leave", I said.

He came in front of me. With a box. My birthday gift. It was wrapped up in a fancy gift wrap. It was so beautiful that I still have kept it. It holds the essence of our love.

"What's this"?

"Open it na first".

I carefully removed each packed corner, I didn't want that gift wrap to be destroyed. I wanted to keep it forever. I still have kept it.

It had a coffee mug. I loved coffee mugs, drinking my favourite cold coffee, in those mugs. But I never bought up a coffee mug, I don't know why. Maybe because it was destined to be a gift from a person whose presence was the gift I would ask for.

"This coffee mug? It's for me"?, I asked

Whenever I used to ask such questions he would tease me.

"No, no for your neighbour", he laughed.

"Whenever you miss me, drink coffee in the mug. You will find my essence, and while you drink the coffee, you can imagine me, and I will feel your lips touching mine, your hands holding my hands," he came closer.

We were all alone. He was with me. I was close to him. But he didn't kiss me because he knew I wouldn't be comfortable and he only came close to me, said bye and I left.

Yes, it's true I have always loved him more than I loved him yesterday but this moment I fell in love with his soul a little more, thinking "kaise mujhe tum mil gaye".

I left him, and rushed to my home.

CHAPTER SEVEN

FACING REALITY

I realised the year was ending, and so our preparations.

Coaching would get closed. Mocks will be the only way to see him. My coaching was now just a mere excuse to see him.

True love never meets you at your best, it comes to you, when you need it the most. If there's anything to me in the universe which resembles the word love, it's losing yourself all in a moment, still being completely, loving someone, selflessly.

I realised, moments are priceless. They never come back.

Moments are personal, the essence wraps you around and the skin smells like an old lavender scent, or like the hazelnut chocolate you love but do not eat often.

// I love you
Sounds so easy to utter
Doesn't it?
But ever thought
About the essence
It carries
how much the words
Can touch a person's soul
Making them mad
Head over heels
For you?

I tell you,
If you love someone

It's never about
Their looks or
Their body
Its about
How pure the soul
Of that person is.
Ah, It's neither about
Lustful eyes
Nor about
Intimate behavior.
    It's not about
lust or desires
That you want to fulfill
But love
Which you set on fire
With a zeal of passion
to love that person
And when,
the aroma of
Care,
Burns all your scars
Making you glow
Just like
A lamp of love
    But darling,
Just understand
Love never demands,
For it's a feeling
Which is too beautiful
To be felt //

I wrote it while I sat on my bed, Comforting myself, penning it all in my diary. Living those moments again. Feeling his glimpse all around.

It was raining and I was waiting for his call when he called me up.

"Thank you for making my day beautiful",I said

"Thank you for making my life beautiful", he smilingly answered.

It was raining. I could feel the sound of showers. Sky was pouring love. Nature witnessed our love.

"You know what I have a do to list, for things what I want to do with you", I said

"Okay.. So tell me about it too", he asked curiously.

"With every phase we will step together, I will tell you those things.

But for now seeing this rain, I just want to enjoy this rain together with you. I want to dance with you in this rain", I said while playing with the droplets.

"We have now our whole life, we will do all things, everything you love doing, we will live our dreams together", he said..

Things were beautiful. We hardly used to fight. We understood each other, we needed no one. But love brings you some pain too.

We enjoyed every moment, and with each moment time slipped.

November came to an end, and so our syllabus.

Institute was going to be closed from mid December.

"Ishq leta hai, kaise kaise imtehaan", the only thing which came to my mind.

My family was strict. Meeting him daily wasn't possible now. But then mocks brought me some relief.

I was upset, so was he. We both were habituated to each other, while I was addicted to him. I realised I became his painkiller and he became my drug. But it could not be changed. It was too late and it would be difficult for me to live without the drug.

Moh always attaches you to the people, it entangles two people together, and to me this song is all about, the pain one goes through when they are ready to hold your hand with the same gravity, you push them away.

Ruhan always knew I wanted to be a novelist. And he was the one who discovered a writer within me. He always wanted me to make a career out of it.

"Shona, why don't you write professionally.
My girl writes so beautifully. The world should know", he used to say.

"My girl"

I used to feel so good when he used to call me his, and each time my heart would flutter and say

"Just yours. Forever. "

"I write for you. I will write someday for the world. But for now you are my world, and you will always be and I love you so much", I used to say.

CHAPTER EIGHT

LOVE WAS IN THE AIR

"My girl"

I used to feel so good when he used to call me his, and each time my heart would flutter and say

“Just yours. Forever. “

"I write for you. I will write someday for the world. But for now you are my world, and you will always be and I love you so much", I used to say.

We used to motivate each other. Entrance was near.

5 months were left for it.

Mocks were going to begin.

December was on its way. But instead of exams, what was bothering me was how I met him.

He was going through something similar.

It was difficult. There have hardly been any days when we did not meet each other. These two years have passed with us revolving around each other.

But there was something more which was bothering me.

We would qualify the entrance and get a college. But now we won’t be together. College in the same city isn’t even possible because his parents wanted him to come to Delhi where they resided and my parent’s first choice was BANARAS HINDU

UNIVERSITY.

Long distance isn't an issue.

Rishton me dooriyan Jaroori hain,
Pass hone ki Kimat samajh aati hai..

But there was a fear, I don't know why. I wasn't trying to overthink but still my vibes were different.

Everything was perfect. Where there were patch ups and break ups, every now and then, we in these months never fought.

Touchwood.

We were compatible with each other..We were comfortable with each other.

Ruhan never failed to bring a smile to my face. Sometimes he used to behave like cute heroes in those Bollywood movies, knowing how filmy I was. He used to love my drama.
He used to tolerate my tantrums. He was always delighted to see me.

At times he used to be with me on video calls, watching me playing with the open hair and sometimes, I used to irritate him by tying it up in a messy bun., just to see his cute face, requesting to free thosc strands. (which was worth it)

"You know I love watching you play with your hair, and when it comes to your cheek kissing you, you look...."

"I look?", I asked

"You look beautiful that I wish I could be those strands of hair, fall on your cheek and kiss it," blushingly hc rcplicd.

"So my man blushes too and my man looks so cute when he blushes."

Months were passing by. We were now talking less. Focused more on the entrances.

But we promised each other that we won't avoid each other any day, no matter what the conditions are, so we always had a little conversation, but 10 minutes would be so little.,

We had so many similarities among us. Reason why we used to call each other soul mates. He was never my boyfriend. He was the boy who was my best friend and the boy I fell in love with.

As the months passed, my fear of losing him held all my heart. We still did video calls after we finished the questions bank.

We gave each other enough time.

But there was a time when I wanted him to see me, love me, play with my fingers. But March was Ending and our exams were closer.

Everyone was now shuffled to batches, according to ranks they scored where revision strategies were discussed.

We were in separate batches.

Biology and maths separated us.

But physics and chemistry unite us.

Those doubt classes were my antidepressants. I could meet him, and this was enough. I realised he was busy studying but I could feel the ignorance.

"Maybe I am just overthinking but my vibes aren't wrong".

April 2017..

Two years before ,I came to know him and I feel lucky to know a person like him

Dates were announced.

Admit cards were downloaded

JEE on 9th April ,

NEET on 7th May.

I still remember the dates.

Exam was closer, very close.

There was fear, we all were afraid.

Chemistry would always screw me up, giving me negative marks, and this would irritate me.

But I was afraid of two things.

Irony chemistry was similar in both of the situations.

"How tough would the chemistry be this year"I used to think each time I lost some marks.

"And how would we be able to keep our chemistry alive in our long distance relationship", a question which I kept in my heart, never asked.

But why did I think of such a long term? Plans hurt. And deciding your future isn't in your hands.

Why I thought it to be forever?

And in thinking of forever, I missed many incredible moments which won't come back.

We haven't talked from 15 days.

Exams were important.

He asked me to not ping him up and just give all the time to study.

But all these 15 days I wrote him a letter each day, keeping it as a draft, avoiding to turn on the net, describing my days.

His JEE paper was over a week ago.

But still 15 days, was yet to complete.

Had I not promised him, I would have just dropped him a text, asking him how his exam went?

How's he?

And keep talking.

But my entrance was still left. And I needed to complete up my mocks.

Days went by.

And finally I turned up the net without acknowledging that I deleted all the letters, and even the last Message.

He read each letter. Each of it twice, replying to me with all the words, which holded his emotions.

But the message he texted was weird.

"Shona I always wanted to be your strength, but I am turning to be your weakness.",

"These 15 days you missed me, and I am lucky you love me so much but, You need to be strong" .

"Nothing lasts forever."

These texts were weird.

I didn't know how to react to these.

Why did he suddenly message me these lines?

But the next very text made me smile.

In all these drafted letters, there was a small text ,which I wrote.

"I really miss you, please milne aa jao na", I said and there my perfect boyfriend agreed , fulfilling my wish.

"Shona, just you and me, let's meet up, may be for a last time"

"Last time?", I asked

"No more questions, let's talk tomorrow. Let's meet.", he said

17th April, 2017

It was our second date. I wore a blue denim, a green sleeveless top and a red shrug over it.

He gave me a missed call when he arrived near my colony.

Blue T shirt, blue jeans, watch on his left wrist, black pulsar, I couldn't realise at the moment what's more hot, his look or the summer.

I saw him after so many days. I kept staring at him for 5 minutes until he asked me will you just keep staring or sit too?

I was bushing

"Where are we going"?

"That's a surprise, my love."

Little did I know it would be the last time we were meeting. He would shift to his parent's place till the results come and counselling begins.

I don't know when we will meet next.

Mind knows it. But deep down in my heart I never wanted to accept this reality.

This was the first time I escaped from my family to meet someone.

The first time I sat on a bike with a guy.

The first time I was riding freely in the streets forgetting out all the fear.

Holding him, leaning on his back. Whispering all much in his ears,and telling him every now and then to look straight. He would turn to look back, smile looking at my face.

It's romantic, until you are not driving.

So I scolded him to look straight on the roads.

I opened up my arms, and shouted out his name as loudly as I could shout.

I started singing his favourite song

"Main tenu samjhawan ki..

Na tere bina lagda jee.", he completed the line

CHAPTER NINE

THE STORY OF FLASHBACKS

As the time passes, my love for you goes deeper and deeper. I had never thought about this. I know you don't love me or maybe you still do.. But still I can't get over you. Whenever I thought of our separation, it left me in tears. I don't know when you became so important to me, but all I know is I found love, peace, feeling of happiness and comfort in you.

While writing this story, my own love story, there were times I got flashbacks, it made me nostalgic but..

Love is not all about commitment, promises, it's also about how reluctantly you want to hold onto the person who is not going to love in return, it's about the confession a person does, and it's also about the memories you decide to live on, even if the person leaves.

Today you are gone, but still my heart craves for you, there are situations I still miss you, I want to call you, share my things out and although i'm broken but still beautiful and strong, strong enough to love you without expectations.

Love can't be measured through metaphors and personification. It's not about the adrenaline rush in your veins nor it's about those poetries we read in school. It's rather about anything and everything, just remember to express it, for maybe your lover is waiting to know how much you love them.

Back to April 2017

With him everything felt so right.

We felt so right.

We reached a silent park. He used to come here very often but I never visited this place, being in this city for too long.

It was beautiful. Every moment with him was beautiful. I was describing to him the struggles all I faced to make my plan work.

He laughed and said,

"Itna kuch bas milne ke liye", he said softly.

"Itna kuch bas tujhse milne ke liye", I whispered slowly in his ears.

I appreciated my guts and my extra efforts to just be with him. I was never into these things. I never lied before but yes I was never in love before.

It created an intangible bond between both of us.

We went to the park and searched for a quiet place. We found a bench. I was sitting next to him. It was all a beautiful dream.

It was all happening in real life.

There was happiness in the air. I never knew these two hours would be the best hours of my life.

It was so magical. Everything felt so good. People go to hotel rooms with their boyfriend or maybe they go to a movie, restaurant or a pub but this was the best place.

I don't know why I never felt earlier. His presence beside me made me forget all the sadness, all what tomorrow will bring.

He was the orange rays of my sun and I was the bluish colour of his sky.

When we used to be separated we were just another colour of a box but when we met we bought a rainbow in the sky.

There was no one near us. It was just us. He kept talking to me about the entrance, his exam, the college he wishes for, and all I did was to keep looking at him,without blinking my eyes even for a second.

I kept looking at him and suddenly felt sensation in my fingers, they now gripped other fingers, leaving out no gap in between.

We got a little closer. We hugged each other passionately, with each other's fingers sliding down.

I suddenly got back and he came closer to me. " Trust me, we won't do anything. Nothing will happen, that we will have to regret.

I know you love me, a little more than I do, and I feel proud to say you are mine.", he said

We were living those memories. He ran his fingers all on my face and I got all into his arms. Grabbing him all and he held me more.

I was breathing heavily. My warm breath could be felt by him.

Everything was perfect.

He was tucking my hair behind my ears, whispering I love you in my ears, kissing my neck and I was losing myself in his arms.

It was all mesmerising. Nothing happened to be regretted. This was real and so was our love.

It was a beautiful moment, and something very memorable.

It was my first kiss. It needed to be perfect. I waited for these moments all my life. Soon, our faces were so close to each other. Close enough to touch each other's lips. He kissed me and I kissed him again, closing my eyes all lost in him.

It's okay if he goes tomorrow, I just wanted to live in the moment. I just wanted to melt myself all in his hand. I wanted him to hold all of me.

The best day of my life, kissing the right person always makes you feel heaven. And he was the right one.

He kissed my cheeks, my hands, my eyes and my forehead.

I kissed him back, taking his hand in mine, holding it. I said, "Even if this world ends I would be happy to have got to know you".

"Shona, listen, I would be shifting to Delhi. I would be there, with you all here. I know you just went out of your way just to be with me, but I don't want you to be so weak.

I always want you to be a passionate dreamer and just not revolve your world all around me.

"Promise me, you won't miss me."

"Promise me, you won't only just think about me. And work for your career."

Promise me, you will love me the way you have loved me forever ", he told me.

"I Anika promise to my Ruhan,in the presence of the sun ,air moon and nature, to love him forever."

"Him", who him?, he teased.

"You, just you, I said with a tear in my eyes. He just held me again, kissed my forehead. He didn't let the tears fall down.

He never made me cry, till the day he was with me.

We shared talks, we shared moments.

We created memories.

I knew this was somehow going to be the last time we were together. I didn't know when I would get to see him again.

I gave him a wallet. The wallet used to carry, maybe still he would carry it . Although he is not mine yet he's still mine.

Why still I get such flashbacks I don't know.

When our relationship was so perfect the bond was so good, Where did it go wrong?

Why even after four years , I'm getting flashbacks?

Many ask me a question and it's absolutely correct.

I have no answers to these.

Nothing lasts forever, and what I all have is his memories, his essence, and my promise.

CHAPTER TEN

LONG DISTANCE RELATIONSHIP

I gave my neet entrance. And in meanwhile,

Ruhan shifted to Delhi. He started to live with his parents.

Long distance relationship was difficult but we started to show effort.

I used to write messages, I used to write poems. Not all poets need to be heartbroken and lonely.

I wasn't sad, nor was I heartbroken.

I was writing in his absence, to cherish my love, divinely. I was in love. He was in love too.

Results came. He decided to take an autonomous college. He scored well but not pretty enough to get admission in an IIT college.

He felt it was our relationship, for he could not make it to IIT and we argued for the first time.

We didn't fight but still I felt a gap getting built up between us for the first time.

We did not talk to each other for a couple of days . And then, my result came.

It gave smoke to the fire.

I scored 366, but the government college couldn't even come into my thoughts. Seeing my score, I decided to prepare for it one more time.

After he got to know my results, he gave all the blame to him, and this relationship for my failure.

"You just thought about me. You thought about our relationship and it got dominated over your career, dreams. I always wanted to be your strength but you made me your weakness".

"My presence won't let you grow", he disconnected the call.

He didn't listen to me. I tried to call but he answered none of them.

I tried all the ways to connect with him, but he was not answering any of my calls or texts. And not even those mails I sent.

He was busy blaming himself for all what happened.

And I was busy accepting all the failures, all my faults, his absence.

I needed him most at this part of my time.

I needed his time, his support, his love, his care but he was nowhere. I was getting used to his absence. Still his absence haunted me.

Why do we live more in metaphors, than in reality? Maybe, because our words hold us to the gravity we love. They talk about the language of love, the seven stages, the theory of unrequited love, but why can't we talk about just letting go. Giving up isn't okay but sometimes it's okay to give up than to hold on and hurt your soul, every single second of life you live

My tries, to get in touch with him were failing everyday.

He left me with no option, to get in touch with him.

I gradually started accepting his absence, still the love wasn't fading. How would it be?

Na wo bura tha
Na usme koi burai thi
Rehna to dono saath chahte the,
Bas kismat ki ruswai thi.

We never fought. He was loyal. We didn't have trust issues. He was caring.

He loved me, I loved him.

Then how could I suddenly fall out of love.

In this chaos, I Spent 6 months where I didn't even know how he was and what he was doing.

He deactivated his social media. His number suddenly got changed, none of his friends knew where he was, or maybe they knew but weren't allowed to send me the information.

I started thinking more about myself, my career was now my priority. But, I used to miss him.

Why did he leave in such a way?
Why wasn't he strong enough to stay?

Earlier I used to write, to let him know what I felt.

After he left, I started writing, to heal myself up.

Love songs were now replaced by the sad ones.

Bin tere became my favourite, and was consistently played in my playlist.

It's been years since we drifted apart, but still when carefree I stand in my balcony to enjoy the drops of rain and the wind blowing all around, I get hitched up by his memories. Your memories still taste like my favourite cappuccino and with every sip I take it makes me addicted to you more.

He was actually a new hope of light, which I always preferred over all the darkest situations of my life.

Though he is now far away from me, still a part of him and your memories always reside within me. He was sweet, funny, crazy, sometimes even stubborn but no matter however he was, he was always acceptable to me and I don't think I'll ever stop loving him.

Sometimes it's not what they show in movies but what actually our heart wants. I believe in the Kafka legacy, over not to accept those who left, but still want to love like our Faraz did.

~ रंजिश है, चाहत है, ये दिल टूटा है तो क्या
दिल भी तो तुम्हारी अमानत है॥

CHAPTER ELEVEN

LOVE, HEARBREAK AND FAILIURES.

Grief is personal, only you can know the profundity of the miseries you've been through. Walking with someone in the rain sounds like a fairy-tale, but what if you're the only one getting wet, while the other person protects themselves under the shroud?

The pain of being left alone is something similar. You're the only one who knows how difficult life gets from the time they walk away from you. Everything seems to fall apart, your dreams, your heart, and significantly you.

A five-lettered word, let go, it's simple to read, but sometimes it takes a lifetime to pull yourself through the darkness and despair you've been overwhelmed with. You remember every minute details about them, what was their favourite colour, how they liked their coffee in the morning, what was their go-to food, and everything else.

But as the time is ticking away, they've learned to live their life without having you around, while you're still struggling to rescue the chronicles of the past, somewhere safe in the crevices of your broken heart.

It takes every ounce of you to recollect all the broken pieces of your heart and place it all in the right place and then gather the courage to love all over again.

I wonder why people are in search of happiness when happiness can be found in all small things.

Everything we do can be a reason to be happy.
From feeling the wet rain drops on your hands, to feeling the winds kissing your face can be the reason to cherish the soul.

From taking a snapshot of the chasing clouds to counting stars can be the reason to be happy.

With every single oxygen we are breathing we are taking a step to our death.

We are losing every precious second of our life.

So let's make a collage of memories with the time which is slipping out of our hands.

Live your life to the fullest.
Enjoy every moment.
Cherish your heart , satisfy your soul.

If you have hundred reasons to be sad,
Find fifty reasons to be happy and the sorrows will decrease.

I started loving my life. His absence didn't break me, yes it broke me, but in a beautiful way. I started to find strength in his love.

In the days when I started to heal myself, I realised I always wanted to be a writer. It was Ruhan who discovered what actually I wanted to be in my life.

I started to scribble with a hope that one day he will read my writing and know if he ever turned the pages of my life, he would know what actually he means to me.

There were days I kept listening to the same song writing whatever was in my heart

//है क्या ये जो तेरे मेरे दरमियाँ है
अनदेखी अनसुनी कोई दास्ताँ है//

There are nights when we are sleepless, where we are neither happy nor sad, broken yet beautiful, trying to find out what it was all about, was it you and me and our unheard story or something that we did not understand.

This song still makes me feel high, as the song starts, it perfectly tunes out my heart, discovering out the reasons why it all ended suddenly portraying to me that we were never meant to be.

Bin tere, a song which just calms out my soul making me realise it was all beautiful, when I was with you.

And makes me cherish the bond we shared, the secret we revealed, the happiness we found, but all this just diminished the moment you left my hand, and went away.

//राह में रौशनी ने है क्यूँ हाथ छोड़ा
इस तरफ शाम ने क्यूँ है अपना मुहं मोड़ा
यूँ के हर सुबह इक बेरेहम सी रात बन गयी//

When I was with you I was happy. Just being with you made me feel the way I never could feel in any other human. The craving for you was different yet unique, for I never experienced this before.

Your presence inspired me each day to be the better version of me.

My heart still aches when while scrolling I visit your profile, and even today it's difficult to accept that we parted and moreover it's impossible to believe that our bond has faded away with time.

It's not the same anymore, we aren't the same anymore.

I still feel lost, there are times I just find myself nowhere, distracted and in a totally different world, trying to be determined not to think about you, I find myself indulged into you a little more every minute.

But then there are memories which still make me happy thinking although we weren't meant to be together, but I was lucky to meet a man like you.

I don't know if it's your absence which makes me spill out the words on the paper or, it was the memories which made me pour my heart out.

CHAPTER TWELVE

CHAPTER THIRTEEN

LOVE IN MY LANGUAGE

Love in my language is like a novel
The one which you don't bother to read between the lines
There's a graveyard, and words surrounds you like a monster
Where the dead leaves, the dry flowers and yes oh Love, how can i forget those dark nights
Where the winds when kissed my face
The heart, now which just know the sound of lub dub, skipped a beat
Similar to the last novel I read.
Love in my language is like drugs
Serotonin which reminds me of an old lover.
The one who resides in me.
She died last night, not even bidding me a goodbye.
It's like inhaling marijuana, sockering the imagery of my mind
And now there's a lover who departed away
Still love is there
The way dried stems wait, even after the flowers withers away.
Love in my language is like the white thick milk,
Dipped out in tranquility of Emptiness,
Feeding much of your insecurities
Unwrapping the possession,
Rubbing your fingers, precisely the thumb over my lips,
wiping out the jealousy it is covered of

It's like a soup, stirred in flavours of
Intimacy /care/love /insecurity /.
To me, at last love in my language is VERMILION
Placed forever to the forehead, defining the love the women holds, and how their husband's name gets to be with them, until they die
But, its not just about a mere relationship,
Rather the sheer love it holds
A sacred knot, tied and where the 7 PHERAS, the 7 VOWS, let you fill all the voids.
Letting you feel complete, not allowing to put out all of your heart
Instead lessening to be with someone at their worst.

Love doesn't always demand to be accepted. Sometimes it's just okay to love someone without any expectations, without any ifs or buts carrying a carefree nature. This song never fails to rejuvenate me, it's been a long time since this song was released, yet it never fails to calm me down, urging me to accept your absence, and just love.It's strange how love fills out all the void, making it look like a perfect story and how difficult it is to be in love. This song describes it all, the pain, the happiness, and the broken promises, in a way which makes it look beautiful, even though it's incomplete.
To love is easy but to fulfil out the commitment is not easy. Love holds emotions and even a courage to let go a person whom you have loved with all your heart out. It's never easy to forget someone who holds all of you, but true love never holds desires, it's how limitless you are to be in love with them.

Everything was in our destiny
Those meetings
Those separations
Those smile
These cries
And that craving temptation
Love dwelling inside two hearts
Neither together nor apart

I repeat, this was all in our fate
In this land of love
In this land of hate
Our two souls met
There existed conditions
There existed desires
It was exactly like love set on fire

My diary was filled with poems, love stories, each prose talking only about him.I never wanted this story to die, now I just wanted to scribble it in such a way that the world starts to hear.
And somewhere my Ruhan reads it.

Can you forget someone who has given you the most beautiful moments of my life, moments which have become memories now, and I feel helpless that I can't make him mine, all I do is cherish those memories that brought us together. Love has its own language, a stage comes when you are still living with their memories when they aren't with you. Where words fail, this song finds a way to make you fall in love with that person a little more than yesterday, and hold onto the person no matter what life brings you.

His love let me speak out in front of my parents, who gave me strength to choose what I really wanted to.

That phase of my life was so unexplainable, being trapped in a situation when neither I could hold feelings, nor prefer to let it go. I hopelessly love those people without any expectations or condition and even when aware that they wouldn't love me in return, yet I cherish them gathering all the scattered broken pieces of my heart.

We met, started conversing and finally I got my special someone in you.

It wasn't easy for me to exist in your life as a friend when my heart was aware that it had fallen in love with you.

Our love story has always been a unique one, it was messy, complicated, and sweet, all at the same time, our meetings, our bond, it was about my unconfessed feelings, which I always hid, because I never wanted to lose you. I wasn't even ready to accept you will ever give up on me.

But it was already mentioned in destiny, the confessions, the urge to stay with each other, the love, and turning our love story into my one-sided love story.

It wasn't easy for me to let you go, but I was determined to never hold onto you forcibly. You didn't love me anymore and I couldn't attempt to make you love me again

It wasn't easy even days before you blocked me, my heart got shattered into pieces, I was mending since the day you went away, leaving behind a void, which can't be filled.

I wish I could text or call you, ask you if you could come back, but I will not.

Honestly, I do still love you, there are feelings which won't fade but then I know that you don't respect me, so what's the use of us being connected, when we don't respect each other. You fell out of love, and that's natural, I could not, because not everyone can move on so easily, especially the way you did.

I still miss you, the memories we cherished, and how happily "us" existed, the past was beautiful, you were my dream comc true, there are days when I get broken into pieces, witnessing panic attacks, feeling depressed, to such an extent that even music failed to give me peace, but then I realised, you have moved on, and what makes me happy is that you are happy, and I should be happy rather than holding on things which won't come back.

The love for you is still the same, at times I just stare at your profile waiting to witness a smile instead of a blank dp but then you never wished to have me in your life, you were never attached after we parted ways, you never tired of holding me back again, and finally, I have decided to make you free, free from my love, free from the guilt of leaving me all here heartbroken.

I know you as a person who gave me a lesson for not making someone an addiction, also as an inspiration for proving myself as a better human.

I have preserved a part of my heart which still loves you, wishes got your happiness, concerns about your health, but not anymore performs the function of dreaming of us together.

CHAPTER FOURTEEN

LETTER TO MY LOVER

Tumhara milna mehez ittefaq hi to tha,
Aur ittefaq se mujhe tumse mohabbat ho gayi

Love is deep, it's about the obstacles, the fights, the boundaries and even about the sacrifices. Not all love stories reach their destination, some are left incomplete, half turned but still are remembered forever.

Sometimes distance brings two people closer, and what keeps the love going is how lovers find peace in the pieces of paper adorned with love, utmost care, and the labyrinth of memories they made. Running your fingers across the words crafted with love, sniffing their scent, tucking it safe in your cupboard so that on days when you miss them, you can read it over and over to feel their love and presence around.

I never wanted to get attached to him in the way I got. He became my antidepressant. The drug I got addicted to. I started to need him just like I needed my coffee. You started to exist inside me, more than my own self. The colours of his love started turning me into a person I was never before.

He rays to my morning, night to my stars, colours to my rainbow, your presence turned my caterpillar to a butterfly. Earlier, I was never into those romantic things, I never liked writing poems about love, but after I met him I changed. I started to describe him in every piece of word ,relieving your memories on all these pages spilled with ink.

Falling for him wasn't easy, it was terrifying. I never wanted to fall in love again but then I met him, and suddenly everything became so different. His presence makes adrenaline rush in my body. His mere presence also started meaning everything and suddenly everything started making sense. Everything with him felt so right. He has been my state of euphoria, my everything I always needed, as if it was meant to fall in love with yourself.

I still have a resolute heart, I still fear emotions but thank you for bringing me things in different light, thank you for making me believe in myself before believing in you, thank you for being there inspiring me

I never believed in miracles, destiny but then I found him, unexpectedly. I never believed someone would complete me, but then he came, and I can hold onto him forever, and all I want to say is wherever he resides, my home resides.

I still wish to say this to him :I love you a lot, all I want to be yours and love you, a little more than yesterday, a little less than tomorrow.

(I wish he reads it all, all the love poems, the one which describes heartbreak too and then which says how much I love him.)

Loneliness can't ever be romanticised; rather it's about how it consumes all your heart leaving a void, maybe the one which can never be filled, asking you to walk on the lane of self destruction.

And it all was unexpected, our meeting, the eye contact, the connection, the talks and even my heart falling for him.
How could he start meaning the world to me?
But then how could I not fall for those eyes which tell a lot without

uttering a word, the smile which cures all my pain, and then when he used to hold my hand the sensation with him felt like the way I never felt before. I fell for him unexpectedly unknowingly.
I never thought he would have meant so much to me that in trying to love him I lost myself.

Ruhan became the reason for my smile, the reason to hold on to things, the reason to try and the reason to believe in love.

He still is the one that my heart craves for, I genuinely love beyond the word love if there is anything other than that. He is the moon to my dark world that is meant to brighten my world.

Love is an unparalleled feeling in the world. Suddenly the words and phrases aren't enough to describe the beauty of your lover. It's undeniable that love changes you as a person, it certainly does. On lonely nights, you befriend metaphors and everything starts to make sense. Their face is like the moon, stealing the darkness from the night and filling up your life with hope and light. Their eyes are like the deep blue ocean you love yourself to drown in and reach to the bottom to unravel the mysteries, one after another. Their lips are like the petals of roses, every time you kiss you plant a piece of yours in them. Love grows eventually, sometimes it takes days, months, or even years to fathom its extremity.

CHAPTER FIFTEEN

THE LAST NOTE

My life is incomplete without him because every second that passes reminds me that you are the only thing that is remaining to make my dreams a reality.

It hurts so bad that each day passes by without you by my side. My heart has always been beating for you, there is no light in my world without you in it.

But then I can't force my love on him .I have always prayed for his happiness and I know I am not the one who enlightens your world.I am not the one who makes you drive crazy like he used to make me feel.

I am not the one and I will never be. Maybe I don't deserve you. Maybe destiny wants it the other way but at least he leads a happy life out there.

You sometimes try to condemn your feelings of possessiveness, suppressing the emotions, the emotions symphonically naming it as mere hormonal balance. But when your heart skips a beat every time you hear their voice, the adrenaline rush never lets you blame it all on hormones. There's a galaxy in your soul craving to find your only moon, for they shine a little brighter making you feel completely the same as it feels when you see a constellation.

You know closure is never a one sided journey but then sometimes you need to decide it for yourself. We often waste many seconds of life in consoling ourselves for unrequited love, broken relationships,heartbreak, and pain. To be in denial is easier than to accept things. Why can't we just accept the things and be happy remembering the moments we once had?

I too decided to write him one last note. To the one who taught me to love, to the one I still believe is mine.

It's been years since I started writing about love, maybe when I even didn't know what love actually is. I was never a person who could put out emotions into words but you taught me when someone falls in love, LOVE becomes their middle name

Love is now my middle name and when everyday the pendulum rotates and gets stuck at 3:00 AM my veins yearn to find your presence and my skin asks to wrap me all in your fragrance.

They say we never run behind to capture a moment until it turns into a memory but no one ever told us that some moments are just beautiful even when they turn into memories. You taught what love actually feels like. You taught how easy it gets to break yourself even when you know if you fall you will shatter. You taught me to fight against all the odds and believe in the feeling. You taught me not to turn selfish yet not to give up.

I know I will never have you , you will never be mine but just remember there's a girl out here who remembers you in her every prayer, and there's someone who smiles seeing your happiness.

I am not the one and I will never be. Maybe I don't deserve you. Maybe destiny wants it the other way but at least you have a happy life out there.

You are with the one who makes you happy, and I am pleased that someone is worth your love. If you ever turn around to look at my world and my love, remember that I am not giving up on you. I will never be happy to love you, and what if you are not mine, I will keep loving you., thinking you are still mine.

And my love for you is like tangent, it touches the circle just once

CHAPTER SIXTEEN

THE END OR A NEW BEGINING?

It's been a long time since I have fallen in love and tried to knit all the emotions of my heart on a piece of paper. My love for him can never be portrayed with the metaphors I write in my poems. What's love? My heart questioned? Was it when my heart skipped a beat? Was it when I looked with the same emotions even when he left?

My letters have always been my podcast of love but today when I look ahead I find not anything in this world resembles ibadat if it's not your name.

After 6 months

I decided to take an arts college, and do what I actually love doing. I decided to be a storyteller, and tell all the stories still engraved in my heart.

Ek tarfa hi sahi ishq nibhana jrur
Hai tumhe mohhabbat unse, ye batana jarur
Wo saath nhi pr tum bewafai na karna
Unse ishq karna, Magar ishq me ruswai na krna

So, I decided to tell our story to this world, because some stories are meant to be incomplete.

Sometimes I just wonder how time changes. I still cannot believe the dilemma that people leave even after the promise "forever " . On one hand people tell you that they are besides you no matter what. And on the other they are the ones who equally bitch about you to people.I never understand the concept of good-byes too. Is it so easy to bid a goodbye by just waving back to the other person? Is it so easy to forget someone who gave you so much to remember, with whom you have created not one, but a zillion memories.

Is your heart ready to let go of all the moments you spent together or is your mind so powerful to forget the person sooner than you even realize that it was not meant to end. I can't understand how two people split all of a sudden out of the blue, especially lately they were the ones busy uploading their pics ,updating their status , publicizing their bond be it friendship or relationship.

While everyone tells me that relationships are a lifetime journey I have witnessed several splits, break-ups, leading to depression and ending up blaming love . When two people come together as a pair or as friends, be it anything for that matter, then misunderstandings, fights are common and natural.

Breakups, misunderstandings amongst friend's are normal but ending up in such a way where the other one just gets lost ending him or herself in depression is not fair. Instead one must try to tackle problems, try to communicate, don't just let your love or friendships go in vain, try the hardest to give all of them a bond.

Because not everyone is as courageous as the person who makes sure to convey their feelings or love the way he or she wants the other person to understand. Someone has rightly said, " To love is very easy, to be loved is difficult."

It's been four years, I do not know where is he

I don't even know what he is doing in his life, there are questions, I need answers about, it's not easy to live here all alone, when there's no conclusion.

Does he still loves me? Is he still mine?

Is he waiting for me, the way I am waiting for him to call? Even today when I get a phone call from an unknown number, I hope him to be on the other side.I don't know why he left. Why so suddenly?
What was my fault or was I not enough.?

Broken heart,
Ripped soul,
Once a love poem,
Now just a hole.
A split couple,
a dead dream

I get low, I start crying going into another zone, I know it's not easy for people to bear my side and nor can I bear it. It's like I am happily sitting with my family and then I just start feeling like depression is hitting me high. I get trust issues, I get insecure and hurt myself, hurting people who really care about me.You know what's worse, when this gets to an extent that people who care about me start feeling suffocated and I make them suffer, making me suffer too. I want to change this side of mine. I know its not wrong to feel low. It's absolutely okay, not to be okay. But behaving in such a way that can hurt your people is definitely wrong.
Love is not all about commitment, promises, it's also about how reluctantly you want to hold onto the person who is not going to love in return, it's about the confession a person does, and it's also about the memories you decide to live on, even if the person leaves. Today you are gone, but still my heart craves for you, there are situations I still miss you, I want to call you, share my things out and although i'm broken but still beautiful and strong, strong enough to love you without expectations
It's hard to forget someone who has given you lots to remember.It's not easy to unlove someone who has taught you to love. There comes a time when they ignore each other.
They try to pretend the others don't exist..
Sometimes it is" Right Love" at the wrong time...

Tute makaan sa ho gya h ye dil,
Na koi tikta hai
Na hi ye bikta hai

Every story doesn't has an happy ending, but some live till eternity. I have waited for him every night, each morning hoping you will come, text, ask about my life, ask about me. It's been four years but you didn't come back. There's everything still your presence can't be fulfilled.I am still calm.

Keeping the flame of forever alive. I know forever is easy to say but not that easy to keep the flame

alive.It's not easy to love with no burden of relationship, boundaries of expectation and loving with free spirit. The endless waits, the path of misunderstanding , the broken promises

the shattered dreams are scary but believe me, It's beautiful, it's beautiful to call him still mine. To still love him. I can still feel his essence everywhere. He is somewhere happy, I can feel he is. Each morning I still pray for him, his happiness, wherever he is, he should be happy.

//Unlike the flowers, autumn and you //

Your love seems to me like a cappuccino dipped in a bowl of chocolate,
With hazelnuts sprinkled
Clumsy, yet asking me to adore
The relationship of flaws with hopes in eyes
Distorted, disrupt,
Still like a story weaved out from above thee universe.

It now asks me not to care
As synonymously care is to breathe
And everytime you left
The touch leaves my heart
Open with vacant pores and voids.

I barely study about quantum,planets, universe, meteor and cosmos but to me your love is like a meteor, burning and shining but it's all dark.

The same way, when you kissed my skin
Giving me erupted feelings
As if the body was numb
Until you pushed the senseless cuticles
The way universe seeks
When two odd couple
Meets

To me you are like the white prism which when touches my body, my soul splashes into 7 beautiful colours,
and my heart searches for the same rainbow every now and then.
It's like crumbled white sheets
Asking for colours to cover my skin with pink
And your love wrapping around it

its never about writing love poems
Rather drinking the poison of love
Toxic yet an addiction to my veins
For love is not just about crimson red
It's about green and blue too
Withstanding for jealousy and possession

It's not always about memorable March,
it's also wittetred flowers, still happening

For you to be my autumn,
unlike the flowers, autumn and you,
and the way my aura witnesses your fragrance just as it notices my love for you.

Life is now like a jumbled piece of puzzle.It has twists, in every other moment.
I Was always like a filmy kid, waiting for my prince charming. Ruhan was like those prince on which fairytales were made, and love is never a fairytale.

He came, he made me believe in love and the one fine day he left, leaving me with unanswerable questions, sorrows, everlasting memories and yes, his essence all around me.

He wasn't wrong, he knew I won't ever stop loving him, I haven't yet but his absence made me the writer, I always wanted to be.

Four years is a long time, but how to forget the promises in his absence, which I promised when he was there with me.For these 4 years, I wrote a letter to him on each friendship day, Isent on his mail, he probably doesn't uses it now, so I never got back a reply, but till this story gets a closure, I won't stop sending those letters to my best friend, I fell in love with.

Now, I have become more mature, I now don't lose my patience, the old school girl is somewhat lost. I try to be more philosophical these days, they say it suits an author's personality.
It's been 1460 days, 35040 hours, 2102400 minutes, and..seconds, (I am still a PCB student and calculation is not my cup of tea, even now).

Love stories never die. It lives with you forever.

Our love story is still alive. A part of me still loves him with the same zeal.
He left, his love didn't. It was his love who insisted that I write my unheard story.An untold love story.

Our story didn't have a perfect ending. It hasn't ended yet. He will call me someday. Someday we'll be together, might be in some parallel universe, if not in this world, maybe some other.Yet, this incomplete story is yet beautiful in it's own way.

Life is very uncertain, we don't know what it is going to throw, death is real and so is life, don't keep regrets, enjoy life to its fullest, there's no tomorrow.
People love, but when it's written in the pages, everyone falls in love with the story.

Our story was meant to be known, till eternity, forever."This was a story the world should know. Anika and Ruhan, are fictional characters, yet some of this actually happened.", as I finished reading the story, in and closed my laptop, an unknown call flashed on my cell phone.

" Hello,.."

Came the voice, a voice probably I was familiar with, the voice I waited to listen to for the last 4 years.

To be continued....

By Tanya Vatsa (Jha)

Author's Bio

ABOUT THE AUTHOR

Tanya Vatsa,(Jha) (20 years) was born and brought up in the beautiful city Patna, capital of Bihar. Emotionally illogical poetess who tries to weave words, finding solace in her prose, poems and stories.

A selenophile, who loves reading books, writing stories, blogs, and finding her home between the words she writes.

"He is still mine" is her debut novel.

She can be contacted at

tanyavatsa21@gmail.com
@unheard_writer

Printed by Libri Plureos GmbH in Hamburg,
Germany